For the old memories
of my parents
–H.W.

To Max Oliver
– C.M.

ℰ
MAS

Text ©1999 by Claire Masurel.
Illustrations ©1999 by Hanako Wakiyama.

Book design by Madeleine Budnick.
Typeset in Beton.
The illustrations in this book were rendered in oils.
Printed in Hong Kong.

Library of Congress Cataloging-in-Publication Data

Masurel, Claire.
          Too big / by Claire Masurel ; illustrated by Hanako Wakiyama.
p. cm.
Summary: Everyone tells Charlie that his new toy dinosaur Tex is too big to take anywhere,
but he proves to be just right when Charlie needs support at the doctor's office.
ISBN 0-8118-2090-4
[1. Dinosaurs—Fiction. 2. Toys—Fiction. 3. Size—Fiction. 4. Medical care—Fiction.]
I. Wakiyama, Hanako, ill. II. Title.
PZ7.M4239584Tr 1999
[E]—dc21   98-36194
                              CIP
                              AC

Distributed in Canada by Raincoast Books, 8680 Cambie Street, Vancouver, British Columbia V6P 6M9

10 9 8 7 6 5 4 3 2 1

Chronicle Books, 85 Second Street, San Francisco, California 94105

www.chroniclebooks.com

Too Big!

by Claire Masurel

illustrated by

Hanako Wakiyama

chronicle books · san francisco

Charlie and his dad went to the carnival.

They had a great time.

They stopped at the ball pitch. . .

and Charlie won!

He chose the biggest prize of all.

"Isn't this one TOO BIG for you?"

asked his dad.

"He is not TOO BIG!" said Charlie. "He is just right."

True, Big Tex took up lots of space in Dad's car.

Back home, Charlie's mom couldn't believe her eyes.

"Oh my he is so. . .BIG!"

Charlie wanted to be with Tex all the time.

"He is TOO BIG for the living room!" said his dad.

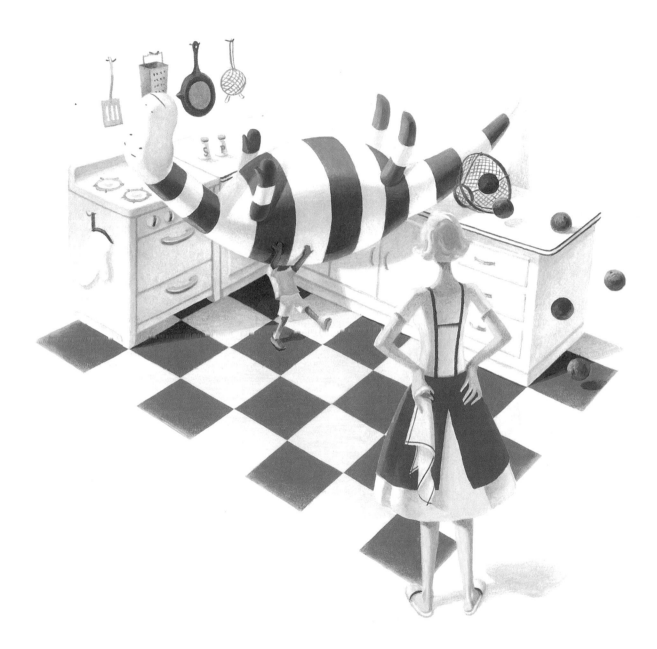

"He is TOO BIG for the kitchen!" said his mom.

Charlie took Tex to his room.

At first Charlie's Teddy and Bunny and
Clown were scared. Tex was so BIG!

But soon they were all friends.

Tex never went to the park.

"He is TOO BIG to come with us!" said Charlie's mom.

"Take Bunny instead."

And Tex never went shopping.

"He is TOO BIG! Let's take Teddy," said Charlie's dad.

grand Cir Clu

Even Charlie's grandma wouldn't

take Tex to the circus.

"He is TOO BIG!

Why not take little Clown instead?"

And so Tex never went to the beach.

He never went to a baseball game.

He never went anywhere.

Poor Tex!

One day, Charlie felt sick.

"We'll have to go to the doctor," said Charlie's mom.

"But WHO will go with me?" asked Charlie.

They looked all around. No Teddy! No Bunny!

No Clown! They were all hiding, just when Charlie

needed them the most.

But not Tex. He was TOO BIG to hide.

He was there and ready to go. Good Tex!

Tex saw the park and the supermarket from the car window.

Together Charlie and Tex read books and
played games in the doctor's waiting room.

Then came their turn.

"Who is first?" asked the doctor.

Tex went first. "Brave Tex!"

Charlie held his paw.

Then it was Charlie's turn. Tex held his hand.
"Nothing serious!" said the doctor.
"But you two must stay in bed for a few days
and take your medicine."

So they did just that. Teddy, Bunny,
and Clown came out of hiding
to keep them company.

"Get better soon," said Charlie's mom,

"and we will go to a movie!"

This time guess WHO went with Charlie?